MOTHER TOLD ME SO

Story by CAROL A. MARRON

Illustrated by GEORGE KARN

A Carnival Press Book Raintree Publishers Inc.

Published by Raintree Publishers Inc.,
Plaza East Office Center, 330 E. Kilbourn Ave., Suite 200, Milwaukee, WI 53202

Art Direction: Jenny Franz

Printed in the United States of America

2 3 4 5 6 7 8 9 0 87 86 85 84

Library of Congress Cataloging in Publication Data
Marron, Carol A.   Mother told me so.   "A Carnival Press book."
Summary: Melissa realizes she is not a perfect child, but believes her mother was one until her
grandmother tells her the truth. (1. Mothers and daughters—Fiction. 2. Behavior—Fiction) 1. Karn,
George, ill. II. Title.
PZ7.M349Mo   1983   (E)   83-7271   ISBN 0-940742-26-8

To Phil, Pat, Amy, Joanie
and, of course, Mother.

My name is Melissa Sue Albina
McCormick.
I am *not* a perfect child.

Perfect children don't drown their mother's houseplants in orange juice.

Mother says I have to sit in my room
and think about what kind of girl would do such a thing.

I only wanted to help.
The rubber plant was drooping,
and the spider plant was losing its legs.

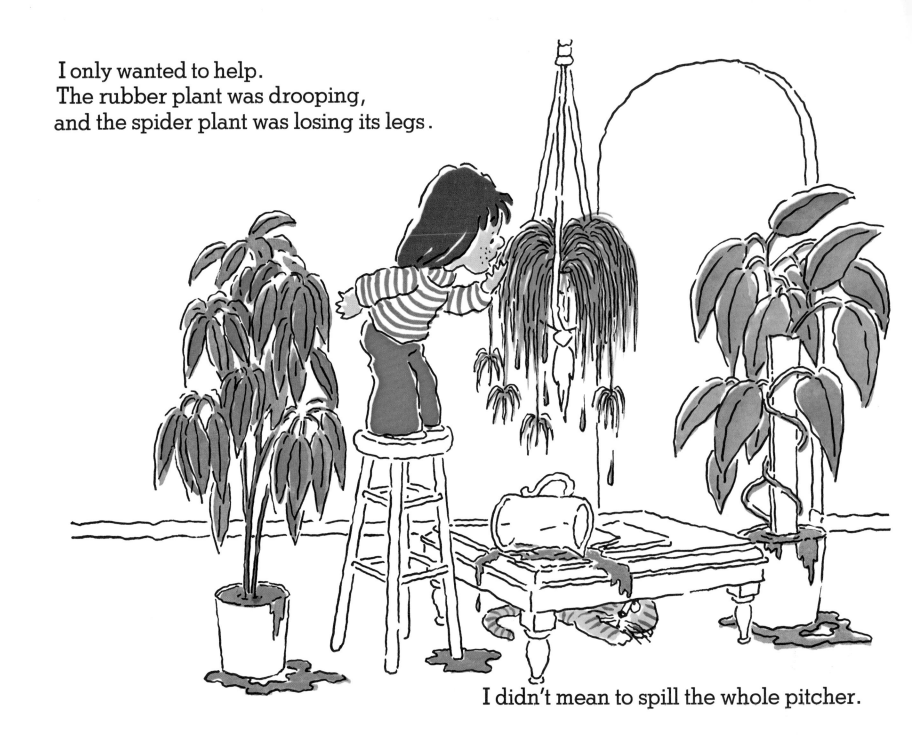

I didn't mean to spill the whole pitcher.

When Mother was young, she would never have made such a mess.

I know, because she told me so.

Mother never spilled oatmeal on the window ledge,

or played slingshot with her scrambled eggs.

She didn't fingerpaint
with toothpaste,

or accidentally flush her vitamins
down the toilet.

Mother wouldn't have slopped
mouthwash on the bathroom floor,

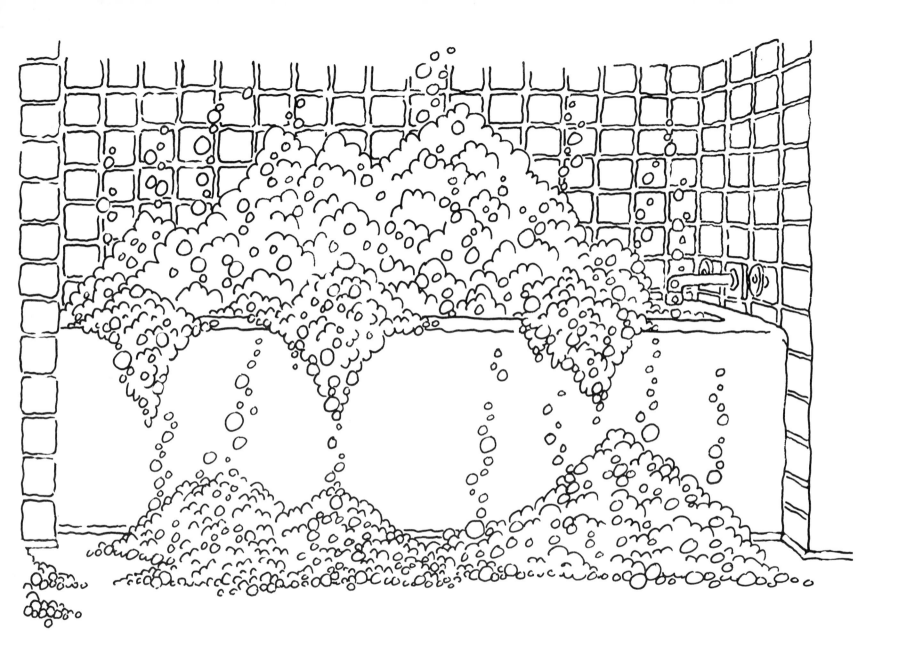

or dropped a whole box of Grandma's bubble bath in the tub.

Mother was *graceful*.

When Mother got ready for school, she didn't
put her sweater on inside out,

or her boots on the wrong feet.

She never played tic tac toe on the apartment walls,
or screamed "FIRE!" in the stairwells.

The only time Mother got stuck in the elevator was when
bratty Percival Barrett pushed all the elevator buttons at once.

I know, because she told me so.

When Grandma and Grandpa took her to the zoo,
Mother didn't get cotton candy stuck in her hair,

or let her balloons float away.

She didn't get caught in
the monkeyhouse turnstile,
or locked in a bathroom stall.

Mother would never have made faces at the gorilla,

or leaned over the alligator pit.

And, she never ever threw up on the Ferris wheel.

Mother says she was a *perfect* child.
But I know better. Mother was a *scamp!*

I know about the snake she hid in her stocking
drawer, and the frog she put in Grandpa's shaving kit.

I heard about the time she stuck
bubble gum in the mailbox slots

and sailed paper airplanes
off the fire escape.

I found out she locked Percival Barrett
in the boiler room

and threw her new school shoes down the garbage chute.

When she was my age, Mother stashed a whole gallon of strawberry ice cream in the clothes hamper,

and turned everyone's underwear pink.

And, one hot afternoon, when no one was looking,

Mother snuck outside,
crossed the street,
ran to the park

and jumped into the fountain...

...WITHOUT ANY CLOTHES ON!

I know, because *Grandma* told me so.

Carol Marron lives in Minneapolis with her husband and three children. She studied children's literature at the University of Minnesota and, in 1979, started an association called The Children's Writers Guild.

Although she is not as clumsy as she once was, her mother still sets out plastic dishes when Carol comes to dinner.

The artist talks about one of his favorite subjects: "George Karn draws with his feet when his hands get tired. He is eminently qualified to illustrate kids' books having gone through many years of childish behavior.

"Although he is old enough to know better, he still thinks as a child; which seems to work very well, except for an occasional spanking."